4 x 4

By

John F King

4 x 4

ISBN 978-0-9931306-8-7

York Europe Publishing 2020

www.johnkinginternational.co.uk

4 short stories x 4 flash fiction
with North Yorkshire associations:

Brief Lives

Fault

V – Force

Voluntary
/

Derek's Last Tape

Moorish

Pedestal

The Last Laugh

+ a Prose Plaque : To the sands of time..

Author photo, Whitby 2019 photo ©ADL

Eskdale / North Yorkshire Moors 1988

4 x 4 +

John F King

York Europe Publishing 2020

ISBN 978-0-9931306-8-7

Brief Lives

York, Railway Station.

Here I am!

I am sorry it has been so much time before writing to you my first letter.

When we said our goodbyes at the *Hauptbahnhof* – I must say railway station - I didn't understand why you think coming all this way a good idea. The journey was long, the people warm but the place cold.

It would not be kind to mention the food in my first post card.

But how are you, *Mutti* and *Vater*, mum and dad. I don't want you to think I am only interested in myself. I know you always want to do what is best for me so this must be the best. But I do miss you.

Let me know your news as soon as you have time. Christmastide is coming!

Your ever loving son

Alfons

PS

The date and address must always head the correspondence. What would they think of me in the *Hochschule*!

York 1938

Dear mother and father

Yes, that is what I have learned to call you. Today we had snow and I joined some other children and we went sledging. The children have made their own sledges. We pull the sleighs - to the top of the city walls and down we go. So fast. I really enjoy it. No it is not so dangerous but I must be careful of my hands. Some of the older boys boast of sledging down a mountain far across the county called Blue Bank but such adventures are not for me. Did you know you have sent me to the biggest county in England. Of course you do.

Tomorrow we will sing carols — We are going to a cathedral at 3pm. Please play along with me in your orchestra. I am sure I will be able to hear you.

I will write and tell you all about it.

Do not work — or play - too hard and make time to write to me.

Your ever loving son

Alfons

Here is a picture of the church. It is called a Minster, St Peter. It is beautiful. The boys in the choir sing like angels. They are not accompanied by string instruments like the ones you play but by an organ that thinks it is an orchestra. The music climbs into the air.

When they sang *Stille Nacht* I closed my eyes and thought I was still at home.

What a beautiful day. Except you were not here. Can we all go together next Christmastide. Promise? I'll have that in writing.

A

Snowed in!

We have food and coal and are snug as they say - *gemutlich* must be the word – winter here is not different to home. I like winter holidays but summer is best.

We have not been out very much. The family here have a gramophone and we play records of the same music at home. German composers – Brahms, Beethoven, and Father York plays Chopin on the piano and Mother York plays Mendelssohn. They are good but not as good as you of course. If you came we would have a full orchestra or at least a sextet: Mother and Father York, Mother and Father real, me and Hilda. She lives next door. I can hear her practising Viola through the walls. She is not that good but I know you wouldn't like me to say that. I think she needs lessons. You could teach her the way you taught me.

What do you think?

A

First day at the new school. It is not easy. The boys and girls are very friendly. Only one boy made sport of my accent but the teachers are kind. I am learning about a group called Quakers. From what I understand they have many good ideas.

It is in the Bootham district of York. I think York is not as big as Berlin but like all cities it is divided into districts. I can travel by bicycle from Bishophill, where we live, across the river, past the great church to Bootham.

One of the teachers welcomed me and said I can stay as long as I like. What shall I tell them? A

I made this postcard myself! I took a photograph of the Church. Father York told me in this city there is a church for every Sunday and a pub for every weekday but we don't go to churches – except of course for music – or pubs! I promise.

Promise you will write to me soon. What news of your orchestra? What is your repertoire these days? It will soon be spring – a busy time for you.

A

At school I am doing well. Should I send you my report? I am top of the class in German! The teacher asked if I would be so kind as to stay behind for extra lessons. Sometimes I cannot tell when the English are making jokes. The English master said try to be top of the class in English and bottom in German. I have done well in music as you would expect of me. I played Mendelssohn *Spring Song* op62/6 at the school assembly. Another boy called me precocious. I said thank you. It is important to be polite.

Love as always, Alfons

Yes, it is important to be polite and you are being quite rude I think. I have been here all this time and you have not written to me once. What am I to think?

Yours sincerely

Fred Greenwood

I am so deeply sorry. I should not have written what I did in my last card. I am ashamed of myself . After all you do for me. You are parents, you are musicians, you must be so frightfully busy. Please forgive me. Write when you can.

Your ever loving son, Alfons

Today Hilda came 'through the wall.' Or to be literal up the garden path. We invited her to tea. I could not believe my ears , or eyes. She plays like she is – beautiful. She must practice so hard – at her playing. While we were taking tea and eating Yorkshire cake – I am told it is called Parkin – Hilda told us of her great adventure. She travelled from York to the capital London by the great express *The Flying Scotsman*. She went with her family to a Henry Wood Jubilee concert at the Royal Albert Hall for a premiere of a work by English composer Vaughan Williams. Is Mr Williams in your repertoire or does your orchestra only play the great German and Austrian composers?

When the time comes for me to go home I would like to go on this train and hear music by this composer. If you don't take me I will wait until Hilda and I are older and go with her.

A

PS I am sorry, of course I would rather go with you.

I am so glad the days are getting longer now. It is bright when I set off and return from school and do not need to worry about my bicycle lamp batteries any more.

It will soon be end of term. I am beginning to understand that this is what you wanted for me – some time in an English school to perfect my education. Of course I have applied myself to all the studies. I did not know the English were so musical. I have learned so much but I think it is time to come home soon?

Let me know how your plans for my return are progressing.

A

I miss you. If you don't write to me I am not going to write to you. So there.

There won't be any more pictures on my cards – from now on they will be like you: blank.

I am so sorry.

It must be the height of the concert season for you and you may be touring Europe.

Here is a picture of the great train I hope we will all go on one day in the not too far future.

THE FLYING SCOTSMAN
LEAVES KINGS CROSS AT 10AM EVERY WEEKDAY

We are having a mid summer celebration. Isn't it wonderful.

Mother and Father York are taking me and Hilda (her family has given her permission) on the train to the coastal town of Whitby. Hurrah! We will go on the beach, watch the fishing boats and I am going to try fish and chips.

I wanted to tell you more about our day trip to Whitby. It was terrific.

But perhaps it is not the right time. I am not telling tales but when I came into the front room today Father York was sitting next to the wireless. He was listening so intently he didn't notice me at first. I think the voice on the wireless was Mr Chamberlain. As you know I am so busy with my music I do not pay enough attention to world affairs. I know it is remiss of me. You taught me it is rude to not let people know when one enters the room. I said good day to Father York. I have not seen him look like this before. I do not like it. He tried to immediately retune the wireless to a Light Music programme. As he moved the dial I am sure I heard some shouting in German.

The atmosphere in the house has changed.

I implore you to write to me. Yes, I do.

A

Hilda and I are taking action. We want to bring brightness to the people we love. How do we do that? Music, naturally. So here it is our concert programme:

Overture: R Wagner: Siegfried Idyll a recording from Berlin by the Philharmonic Orchestra conducted by W Furtwangler

Piano interlude: Spring Song by F Mendelssohn played by Alfons Grunewald

V Williams: Serenade to Music , a recording from the Abbey Road studio London by BBC Symphony Orchestra conducted by Sir H Wood.

Viola interlude: Märchenbilder by R Schumann played by Hilda Earnshaw accompanied by Alfons Grunewald

World premiere: original composition by Alfons Grunewald 'Love is a Journey' for piano and viola, performed by A Grunewald and H Earnshaw.

Finale: Beethoven Ode to Joy, a recording by the BBC Symphony Orchestra conducted by Sir A Boult

Tea will be served.

Yes, we want to bring brightness to the people we love. That means you.

If you don't come we won't play.

Final.

To: City of York Library and Archives, United Kingdom

From: Ministry of Culture, Czech Republic

Esteemed colleagues

I am writing to you at the request of our President Mr Havel.

Following reorganization of our archive additional effects concerning the Terezín camp and ghetto of the Nazi are available in the public domain.

We have the pleasure of returning the following documents to their city of origin-

Post cards sent to Herr and Frau Grunewald from Mr Alfons Grunewald

Drawings of British cultural, rail and port installations attached to certain post cards

Manuscript of concert programme attached to post card sent by Mr Alfons Grunewald.

In addition we are in effect forwarding to you-

Letters withheld by Nazi authorities addressed to Mr Alfons Grunewald of York by Herr and Frau Grunewald from Terezín.

Manuscript of concert programme enclosed with one of letters by Herr Grunewald. This document was written by Herr Grunewald to be sent through the offices of the Red Cross but was withheld by Nazi censors possibly on grounds that the programme contained unlisted English music (by Mr R V Williams) and is dedicated to Miss Hilda Earnshaw of York.

Herr Grunewald was deported from Terezín to Auschwitz January 1943 and Frau Grunewald October 1944.

If we can be of further service please do not hesitate to contact us.

On behalf of the President of the Czech Republic, 1994

To: The Editor, Second Generation Voice 1996

From: York University Music and Drama Soc

Please could you include in your listings this programme of music and readings to be performed by members of the university music and drama societies at York Minster on 27 January 1996 for *Gedenktag für die Opfer des Nationalsocialismus*

V Ullmann: Autumn

Introduction: Dr Hilda Earnshaw

Readings of selected cards and letters by the Grunewald family.

R Vaughan Williams: Serenade to Music

A Grunewald: Love is a Journey

F Mendelssohn: Spring Song

'Ladies and Gentlemen.

Welcome. Some of you will know me as the former Professor of Music at the University, many of you will not. So firstly an introduction, why should I, Hilda Earnshaw be invited to talk with you at this event for 6 million.

 I will be brief, this is not about me.

My name was almost Hilda Grunewald. The 'almost' in that sentence was inserted by Nazis.

My fiancé Alfons Grunewald was killed in an air raid on York, April 29 1942. I was the girl next door. Alfons Grunewald was sent by his parents to York by Kindertransport. He came from and to a musical family. He was a gifted pianist and potentially a great composer. Each of the years he was in our city we held a soiree in Spring and Autumn in the house of his or my York family. That spring it was at my house. The house next door, the house where he had travelled to be safe was destroyed by bombers.

Unbeknown to us his parents' orchestra were giving a concert that very evening. In Theresienstadt.

I have never particularly used words like almost, potentially, fate or victim, even though this day uses the word *Opfer* in its title. Perhaps one day we will have a different title, maybe Holocaust Memorial Day would be appropriate.

I do wonder why the Nazis so disliked Alfons as to bomb him as he went home after our concert and murder his parents and the orchestra after theirs.

All they ever did was play music.

And that dear friends is what we will do today.

Brief Lives by John F King, 2GenerationNetwork. 4x 4

It's Your Fault, This Happened.

'BBC'

'I must have the wrong number'

'Beyond Belief Communications'

'Right number'

'Right call'

'I was advised you are the best in the business.'

'Yes'

'So are we, let's not waste any more time. I want to set up a meeting.'

'Immediate agreement there, no time wasting, anything else you want to talk? Name, Money?

'I assure you it will be worth your time. Financially, professionally.'

There was something in his tone that sounded convincing. I ought to know. It had always been my business model to land one big contract and dosh in rather than shoals of mini-contracts and burn out. That is why I set the business up. BBC. Beyond Belief. PR, media, communications. At least a double meaning in the title I know. I never do things by chance.

'When, where, who,' I said. I hoped my tone mirrored his.

He gave me name, sat nav coords. I almost expected him to say something like 'alone, no fuzz, nothing.' He didn't.

'6AM? Good for you?'

'I have a 5.30', I said, 'sure I can squeeze you in.' I hate being last worded as much as I hate 6AM. One of the reasons I set up my own business was no joker could say to me 'breakfast seminar' ever again, croissants as stale as the air, undecanted Tropicana. Class.

5.45 AM. I stayed in the car and check the coords again. It was definitely correct, it was definitely deserted. Maybe I should have told someone where I was going. Maybe not. I looked around me as the windows whirred down. I could hear the sound of a river, across on the far bank, a blue flash. A bird I recognised from a logo I studied for an alcohol account years ago. Kingfisher.

The bird stared straight back on me. I couldn't take my eyes off it either. A distant noise and it was gone. A vehicle drew up parallel beside me so we were driver to driver.

'Beautiful, isn't it,' he said. 'Follow me.' We convoyed along the river bank for 6 minutes and stopped in front of a security link fence. He flashed a card at an electronic reader and we went into a compound.

'I want you to sell this, he said.

There was nothing there. 'It's hard to sell nothing.' I said.

'Patience,' he said.

I looked again at his business card. Frank Welt, CEO Hydro Move.

'Call me Frank , he said, 'same time tomorrow.'

'Let's talk now, tomorrow is another day.'

'I'll start your account as of now. Firstly I simply wanted you to come, See things as they are in the now, see for yourself before..

'Before what?

'Before tomorrow.'

I had three minutes between appointments that afternoon in the office. I googled Hydro Move. There were photos of the river bank with the Kingfisher. I was trying to find deeper links when the desk phone went.

'BBC.'

'Sorry I must have the wrong number.'

I was beginning to think the ambivalence wasn't as neat as I thought. I said

'Beyond Belief Communications'

The silence at the other end was confused before recovering to

'I'd like to speak to Mrs Nadia Jenkins-Snell. Personal matter.

'This is Ms Jenkins'

'This is the headmistress of Eskdale School. We have had a serious incident involving your son. I would be grateful if you could come into the school immediately.'

I thought I'd seen something unusual about the photos on the Hydro Move feed.

'Can this wait? I'm in the middle of something at work right now.'

'So am I.' The headmistress had this headmistress tone. I didn't like it.

'Have you spoken to my ex-husband on this matter?' I said, let the loser deal with it, I didn't say.

'We endeavoured to contact your husband and only have a voicemail and an out of office reply.'

People who say endeavour mean they haven't tried but I could hear she wasn't going to go away.

The drive to the school took longer than expected. I managed to overtake one lorry only to get stuck behind another. When I arrived at the school car park the car was covered in mud.

I followed the head into a window less room. Dean immediately said

'I didn't do nothing.'

The head spoke over him.

'Your son was involved in a physical altercation with another student. He is accused of bullying, alleged assault. It is a serious incident.'

'I didn't do nothing,' said Dean.

'He said he didn't do anything,' I translated for the head.

The head appeared to be reading from some kind of report.

'During a Climate Day..'

'Climate Day?'

'Yes, students are allowed to hold one climate day a month, they can design their own placards, devise slogans, debate but not leave the school premises. One of the other students was holding a placard at the school gate. Dean approached this student, took her placard and attacked her with it.'

'What did the placard say?' I said to Dean.

My phone rang at 5.30 AM next morning. What have I done to deserve this? It wasn't Frank Welt requesting a lie in but my Ex. We don't live together anymore for Dean's sake but I'm too busy for divorce proceedings.

'What do you want?' I said.

'Good morning Nad,' said Giles.

'What do you want?'

'Dean texted me. Said someone annoyed him at school. Seems to have ended in a suspension. For him. I can take him today if he is still off school.'

'What's in it for you?' I said.

'Don't mention it,' he said. 'I'll pick him up later. Incidentally, why were you already awake?'

'Doesn't concern you anymore.'

The kingfisher looked at me again that morning. In the same way, not friendly not hostile. We were simply there.

'You're late,' said Frank. It was 6.09AM

'Your fault,' I said, ' stuck behind one of your lorries. Let's get on with it.'

We were there for the contract. What is the message, what are the channels, what is the fee?

'Put these on.' Frank offered to replace my heels with a pair of Hunters. 'We'll walk and talk.' Frank outlined his picture of the brief. The fee was even by my standards outstandingly high. If I was in business to say ' what's the catch' I would. 'What I want you to do,' he said 'is to normalise what I do. Reach people who have already made up their minds.'

'About?'

'This.' In front of us was a wide gate, painted forest green. I hadn't noticed it until he flashed a kind of credit card and it began to open. I t was like a movie set. An endless field had turned to mud, there were lorries and trailers everywhere, men in hard hats, floodlight towers. There was still no noise. I was about to make a comment enquiring if this was a site for people to break into or out of. Something in Frank's manner told me it wouldn't be well received.

'Fracking,' I said.

'No, Fracking is not a word we – you – ever use. This is Hydro Force. We extract the shale gas our surveys have found beneath here by hydraulic fissure. We can supply all the local urban areas and export surplus through Whitby and Teesside. It is the best thing to happen to this area since…

'Finish your sentence,' I said.

'When we have extracted everything the site will return to as it was the first day you came here. Call it natural gas. Actually with what I'm paying you call it what you call it. Except..

'Fracking.'

'Good lady', he said. I let this go. 'I want you to make us the real friends of the earth. Can you do it?'

She who hesitates is lost. 'Yes,' I said.

'Sleep on it. Back here 6 AM tomorrow. Sign the contract, first instalment in bank of your choice.'

'Upfront?'

'What did you expect?'

I wanted to get back to the office straight away. Brainstorm slogans, do some reverse thinking, fracking had such a bad image turn it round. Do you remember that pack of cigarettes that had a skull and crossbones on it, when cigarettes still had images on them? Yet my journey back took even longer than the trip out. I sounded my horn at a convoy of vehicles in front. They were like something out of Mad Max and probably didn't pay tax either. The vehicle at the front, a rust heap with a chimney in the roof pulled over. A man emerged and sauntered over to me and tapped on my window.

'Why are you in a hurry?' he said 'are you going to some sort of emergency? Do you not appreciate the beauty around you?'

His voice was difficult to place, sort of Archers walk on meets media studies lecturer.

'I haven't time to talk to you,' I said.

'Don't you care about the planet?' he said, tapping the body of my Cayenne. 'What do you care about, why do you have no time?' the man was unsettling me, not because I thought he could use the Frankenstein style bolts he had shot through his visible anatomy to 'key' the car but because…because what?

I reversed the car the way I came, the only way out. Past the slid back green gate to the T junction with the main road. From one direction lorries with heavy lifting equipment were trundling in, from the other Mad Max vans, tricycles, gaggles of walkers, more like those you see on 'Text UNICEF' posters than Ramblers Holiday ads.

I would still be there now if a flash car hadn't flashed me to let me out but then indicated I should pull over. Dean emerged from the non drivers seat, Ex from the other.

'Grow up,' I said to them both.

'Don't mention it,' said Ex 'where are you heading?'

'Office. You?'

'We're working too,' said Dean.

'Looks like it.'

'Test driving the Tesla. Zero emissions. 0- 97km/h 1.9 seconds.'

'You must be busy.'

'Have you seen them? The anti Frackers. We want to interview the guy in the van with the chimney upfront. Stringing the story to regional news, hopefully nationals. They are going to start tomorrow. Thought Dean could do some vid work. Make himself useful on his sabbatical.'

'There is no fracking here,' I said.

'No fracking, mum! Thought you were supposed to be really on it,' said Dean.

'You stay out of trouble Dean, back to school tomorrow. Your father is a bad influence.'

The now familiar drive to the site of the sliding green door taking twice as long, the road traffic doubled by the strange shapes of vehicles of the Hydro Move contractors and detractors.

It was still dark when I left home to be on time. Immediately I signed the contract Frank pressed a button on his mobile twice. An alert vibrated on my mobile once.

'Breakfast?' asked Frank 'celebrate mutual interests, Hydro Move and Beyond Belief. I think you should have something to eat. You look like a black coffee type.'

I wasn't sure how to take this. 'Lost for words?' said Frank, 'not the best start for my Head of PR. A smile came to his face. 'Let's go Dutch.'

We walked to a portacabin. Inside it was kitted out as a canteen that could obviously deal with large numbers quickly. 'Quantity and quality' said Frank in answer to my look. He said to the man behind the counter 'full English' and turned to me 'and you?'

'Usual,' I said

When his breakfast arrived I looked up and said 'So you are not planning on staying on this planet too long?'

'I'm sorry?' he said. It was the first time the optimism had slipped off his face. I indicated his plate, a parody of a fry up. He looked at my mug of black coffee.

'I'll live longer than you, when I go the planet will be a better place.'

The double meaning seemed stuck on his plate.

Frank said 'When can I see you again? I mean for you to present your strategy.'

'Not sure I can cope with more of these 6AMs right now.'

'6PM. Dinner. I'll message you.'

Instantly the green gate closed behind me a hellish noise started up, floodlights more intense than you can see in any war film beat the dawn.

I stopped the car by the river bank where I had seen the blue bird. I checked my phone alone. A massive amount of money had been deposited in my company account from a bank I had never heard of.

From 10 the next day the office phones never stopped ringing. The accountant said an unusually large sum of money had been deposited in the company account from a bank in the Dutch West Indies. Was I aware of it? Yes. A non call from my estate agent giving me a 'heads up' on imminent market movements which could be 'up or down' but I should move fast.   Printer discussing shades of blue for the Kingfisher logos. Personal call from Ex wanting a face to face.

'Can't we do this over the phone?' I said. 'I'm busy.'

'With what?' he said.

'We don't do pillow talk any more.'

'We never did' he said.

I gave him a slot late afternoon. I could honestly say I had an appointment at 6, he understood deadlines as a journalist though he never had as a partner.

'Who are you seeing?' he said.

'What do you want to see me about?'

'Why did you lie to our son?'

'I didn't. I don't.'

He mimicked my voice, at least I think he was, do you know what your own voice sounds like? 'There is no fracking here.'

'There isn't'

'There is.' He flourished a centre spread of The Yorkshire Post. Under his by-line photographs of the Hydro Move site, the vehicles. Revealed beyond the wide open green gates an operational rig. 'Look and Learn' style graphics of the shale gas process. On the page opposite interviews with the man I recognised with the bolts through his neck under the heading Climate Emergency and the caption in bold ' How Green Was My Valley.' Ex looked pleased with himself.

'You managed to do this all on your own?'

'Dean took the picture and pulled up the graphics.'

'It's a family affair,' I said.

'Would have been if you hadn't ruined it,' he said.

'We've been through that. If you want to present your angle I know a good PR company. What are you here for? I told you I have an appointment.'

'Dean's been expelled.'

'It was his first day back. I thought you had that covered.'

'He hit someone. Again. Harder.'

'Why?'

'He must have been angrier.'

'What did he say?'

'Dean said mum lied, there is fracking.'

'It is Hydro Processing. There is no fracking.'

'You and your words.'

'You and yours.' I screwed the newspaper up and gave it back to him.

'You can wrap your fish and chips up in it. Dean is with you for dinner. I have to go out. Now.'

Frank Welt might not like reading press over breakfast before I could get my logos all over the story. Second instalments from offshore bank accounts can be stopped in a click.

'No,' said Ex, I have to go out, you need to sort Dean.'

Welt's phone was going straight to Voicemail. I rang the number given on the corporate web site. A woman's voice answered first in Dutch then in English:

'Hydro Move. All media enquiries are welcome by our Amsterdam Communications Team.'

I left the office on the route I knew so well. I never got beyond the river. It was a bridge too far. At this side police control vehicles, at the other hippies or other weirdos. Schoolkids in same uniform as Dean modified arrived in a people carrier covered in amateur slogans but stayed in the vehicle with the engine running. A rear window opened, I saw the weedy speccy kid who had provoked Dean throw a packet of Walkers out. The window closed, their slogans lost to condensation.

My window wound itself down. A WPC leaned in. 'No public access beyond this point. Safety.'

'Isn't that the public over there?' I asked. 'I have a right to go about my business.'

'Which is?'

'None of yours.'

My window wound itself back up.

I left another Voicemail for Frank: ' Frank, so sorry I can't make dinner. How about…' The voice mail was beeping full. I uploaded the Kingfisher logos from the car.

Back at the office Dean had his Reeboks on my desk, playing with my PC.

'Thought you'd be pleased to see me', he said, not looking away from the screen.

'I need the computer. Now would be good.'

'Cool.' He left the cascade of screens open. On one a group of - 'what do you call these people ?' I said to Dean. 'Hippies, activists, idealists?'

'Losers,' he replied, ' especially those two. I mean you put me on the planet to embarrass me?' On the screen Ex was holding his iPhone up to Mr Pierced through the Nose Media Studies Planet Saver in some kind of All The Presidents Men press way. The WPC appeared to be asking them to move back, apparently at this angle at the instruction of an official in a Hydro Move vis jacket with a walkie talkie.

'Have you sent this to anyone?' I asked Dean.

'Not yet.'

'Don't.'

'What's in it for me?'

'Nothing.'

'OK, I'll press send then.'

'Wait.'

'What's in it for you?'

'Money. Big shed of.'

 Dean looked up. 'What's for dinner?'

'Fish and chips.'

'Again'

'Chips and fish. What is going on with you, Dean?'

'Nothing.'

'These are fresh peas, not mushy. Why can't you do anything properly?'

'Don't mention it.' I heard myself say. I spread the fish, chips and peas out from a back issue of the Whitby Gazette over the upturned unpacked packing crates. 'At least I don't go around hurting people.'

'Don't you?'

'Meaning?'

'You take money from anyone to say anything. You smashed up the home you were never in. You're a nihilist.'

'Language, Dean.'

He flicked the TV on without asking. '…And now over to the news where you are.'

Ex was standing with bolt man in the middle of the river bridge. On one side you could see the police vans with their wire mesh cover windscreens and the inevitable Tesla. On the other a motley collection of cronky motor homes blocking a Hydro Move truck. 'Let me be clear,' Mr Bolt was speaking ' Hydro means water. Hydro Move means oil, gas, disaster. They are nihilists. They think we are fools. You can't put a Kingfisher logo on an oil and gas rig. They think local people can be falsely bought. Not everyone is a nihilist.'

I looked at Dean: 'Smart kid like you getting expelled from school?'

The tv ignored me ' I'm sorry we don't seem to have the feed for this package. I'll hand you back to the studio…'

Dean said to me 'don't mention it.'

I let Dean sleep in the next day. The first call I took in the office was from the accountant. The bank in the Netherlands Antilles had been instructed by Hydro Move International to withhold any further instalment to BBC.

I remonstrated; I'd delivered the logos and outlined a strategy. 'Water under the bridge' was the reply.

There was no way to spin that day. The headmistress office at Dean's (ex) school eventually returned my call. 'We can see no way Dean is returning to this establishment. Three strikes and out. He has bullied and worse his fellow students. He has attacked students for going on the climate strike, he has attacked students for not going on it. We cannot go into motives, if there are any. We cannot accept him.'

My estate agent returned my requests for an update with more alacrity although the beneficial gap in my favour of moving from London to the North seemed to be daily narrowing. 'This one is a real opportunity. Prime property, new build, hardly lived in, even has a sauna, pre-surveyed, not on open market, ultra-quick sale required, surpasses your spec. I'll hold it off the market for you at 33% below todays market value.' I could do this without Ex, without the second instalment from hydro, without renewing the service apartment. Dean and I looked at the house from the outside.

'Cool' he said. 'At least there will be a table for our fish and chips, a wall for our TV. Can I stay with you Mum?'

'No. You haven't got a proper job, you have been expelled from school and you hit people.'

'I'll work for you. Full time. Someone who understands graphics, vids, feeds, whatever.'

'What about Dad?'

'I'm not living with Giles.'

'Is that his name? Why not?'

'Why not?'

'Like he's under some kind of illusion he's cool. At his age. Gross.'

'And me?'

'You're cool.'

'Why's that?'

'You don't believe in anything.'

The new house gave us a shorter ride to the office. I was surprised at Dean's capacity for early mornings.

'BBC' Dean answered the phone. 'It's for you, international,' he said in a semi-professional voice.

'Beyond Belief Communications.' The pause was nearly creepy long. I was about to hand the phone back to Dean.

'It's Frank .'

'Frank. I thought… let me explain. About the dinner, I was on my way but…'

'I only just found out it was you.'

'What?'

'The estate agent. The house papers, your name. Nadia. I didn't think. I didn't think it would be you, any individual, I thought at that price a company, a builder would go for it, someone who can absorb it. Have you signed, everything come through?'

'Signed, sealed, delivered..'

'It's in the operational zone,' he said, 'What in business we call the zone.'

'Yeah, business zone. Cool.'

'It wasn't your business to understand. The operation. The house is where it shouldn't be.'

'There must be…'

The line beeped and clicked : 'Frank?'

Business slowed that day. We drove home. There was a diversion. We crossed the bridge now surrounded by a perma camp.

'Some people don't have homes to go to,' said Dean.

The WPC halted us at the driveway to our house. A mobile phone mast lay like a January Christmas tree across the gravel.

'Not safe beyond here,' said the PC. There was a Tesla parked opposite with a PRESS sign in the rear window.

Dean hitched a signal from another network, he held up his phone tuned in to a local radio interview. Two now familiar voices emerged, more a double act than interview. One said 'It isn't about sensation, we called Fracking out for what it is, I hate saying 'told you so…it's beyond belief…we only hope people don't get hurt…'

V-Force

'I don't know, Sir.'

'You aren't paid to say I don't know, what are they?'

'I don't know. Could be an exercise.'

'Again. What is the difference between an exercise and the real thing?'

'I don't…I think they are turning back.'

The green dots of the radar screen curved out then broke formation. They were on the right edge of our airspace.

'They are dispersing' I said to Sir. 'All clear.'

'Cheer up' he said, might never happen.'

I never took my eyes off the screen. Our station could only provide a four-minute warning tops, civilisation wasn't a question of centuries but seconds.

'I ordered you to cheer up,' said Sir. The silence wasn't a good one. Sir bombed it. 'I'm thinking of putting you up for an MBE.'

'Thank you, Sir.'

'Interesting response,' he said, 'not why or what does MBE stand for?'

'What does MBE stand for, Sir?'

'Miserable Bastard par Excellence.'

'Thank you, Sir.'

The silence returned, the atmosphere unchanged. I broke it.

'Sir, MBE shouldn't that be…'

'Keep your eyes on the screen' said Sir, adding 'that's an order.'

Sir was correct of course. 4 AM. Time when you least expect it, time when you most expect it.

'Funny, isn't it, Sir?'

'I don't find it funny.'

'I mean time. 4AM. 4 minutes. Kind of neither here nor there.'

Sir was silent for a minute. I thought we would leave it there. He wasn't a man to banter with at the best of times.

Then he said

'You can do a lot in four minutes.'

I waited for him to expand. He didn't. I shouldn't have filled the silence but said

'I suppose you are right Sir. Hit singles are 3 minutes now. That's what I would do in those last minutes, listen to music…'

'MBE,' intercepted Sir.

I failed to eat my yawn. Sir sees everything.

'Right lad,' he said, 'off you pop.'

'But, Sir'— I looked at the wall clock. 'There's still 56 minutes to go.'

'I'll cover it,' said Sir. 'You seem tired, distracted, no use to me. Off you pop. Bed. Straight to. And take 24.' He added 'You never know if each day is your last.'

I don't know where that came from. It didn't feel right to leave it in the atmosphere.

'What would you do if it was your last day, Sir?'

He looked at me as if about to say something. But didn't. Sir was ex Bomber Command. I knew he'd seen some things in his time but he was ultimate stiff upper lip. Once on his fourth half in the mess he began a sentence – reminds me of that time in the kite over Bremen, but the steward called last others and he left with his half half empty.

I protested about leaving him alone on the shift once more.

'Is there a Mrs Sir, Sir ?' It was the most daring thing I'd ever said in the Service. dangerous. 'Someone for you, Sir, off shift, nice full English…'

He must turn round, I thought, I could feel he heard me.

'KBO. Kindly Bugger Off,' he said ' We can't afford any misreading of these blips,' his eyes burning onto the screen. 'Take 24.'

I wondered for a moment if he knew something I didn't. Few people have higher clearance than Sir. We were all briefed as far as possible in the Big Picture but the essential thing in an operation like this is to know your role, do it, do it well, automatically, without question.

Maybe the chief was right. He always was, kind of bloke you'd always follow. I imagined him issuing orders in the bomber over Bremen, 3 engines out, how he'd kept everyone alive, unless you counted those under the open bomb doors of course.

The stress tapped some of the chaps. I was blessed with the ability to kip anywhere anytime. I think it was a blessing, kept me going when others didn't. That's how I was on the shifts with Sir. You don't normally expect the station chief to be sitting next to you in front of the screen, hands, eyes, on.

We started the shift at midnight. I'm not making this up but the chief arrived with a royal crested suitcase handcuffed to his wrist.

'Don't,' was all he said when he saw my eyes flick from his salute to the crest to his wrist and back.

It was 2.32AM when he spoke. A WRAF had brought a brew in. It was a kind of break. My peripheral vision enveloped her retreating figure.

'Eyes, Reginald,' said Sir, never leaving the screen.

Sir was right, as ever, so far. Could I have pushed him - if this was your last 24 hours what would you do? Perhaps I already knew the answer; he'd do what he always did. Me? Maybe I did need a screenbreak. 24 hours. If it was going to happen, it was going to happen. My plan wasn't that different to any other 24 hours leave I'd taken in this part of the world. Some people said live like it's your last day on earth anyway. I didn't agree but I did want to make the most of it.

'How did you come to be called Ingrid?' I said.

'I thought you need to be smart to be in the RAF,' she said, her eyes moving 180 degrees north to the cinema board above us showing ''Casablanca''.

'We'll always have Whitby,' I said.

It was only the second time I'd met Ingrid. I think we both saw this a date without exactly categorising this as such. These were uncertain times. The first time I met her, at the dance in Sleights village – it was equidistant in miles between the base at Fylingdales and Whitby- she approached me directly and said 'what do you do?'

'I can't tell you,' I replied, which was probably meant to be Len Deighton encounters Ian Fleming but wasn't. The second time we met I asked her – What do you do? Her reply was enigmatic.

'You tell me.'

If there was a third time I'd change the subject.

After the other Ingrid decided to board the Dakota we walked up the hill, through the whalebone arch, to The Royal. My second pint was half empty when Ingrid said 'Explain it to me again.'

'It's depressing,' I said.

'If you really think that why are you a part of it?' There was an edge to her voice I hadn't spotted before.

'I do it to keep you safe,' I said without knowing why, 'didn't you understand the first time?'

'Don't patronise me. Tell me again. I want to know if you believe in it.'

'How can you know that?'

'Tone of voice.'

I repeated the theory in what I think is my authoritative voice. You must convey belief.

'No one will attack us because we will attack them. The level of force is so overwhelming, the result so certain it would be mad, useless, illogical to initiate it. There can never be a war because no one would win. As long as the enemy totally believes we will retaliate everything will be alright. Alright?'

There was a pause. After about 3 minutes she broke it.

'Yes,' said Ingrid. 'You do.'

'What?' I said.

'Believe it.'

The silence seemed to go on for an eternity, cloud hung in the air from nowhere. How did we start this? It was my call to disperse.

'Can I see you again?' I said, different tone.

'You're obviously still going for it,' said Sir.

'I'm sorry Sir, not with you?'

'MBE. Miserable Bastard par Excellence. I expected a new man after your leave.'

'Leave? You mean the 24 hours? Sir.'

'Miserable and ungrateful. How was it?'

'What? Sir,'

'The 24. A lot can happen in …'

I retaliated first. 'How was your 24 hours, Sir?'

His eyes left the screen for the first time. They were as red as a fire bell. 'Sir, I began, you should…'

'You don't get to should me, son,' said Sir. 'I asked you a question.'

'Girl. Film, Bar' I replied.

There was a pause while he seemed to stare even more intently at the radar screen. I thought the subject was closed. We worked on in a green silence until he said 'See?'

The dots on the screen were clustered now for what passed as usual. I made no comment to Sir.

'I mean the film, what did you see?'

I wanted to tell him her name was Ingrid but he hadn't asked me.

'Do you like films, Sir?'

He looked at me again. 2.33 AM. I wished he would sleep. I wish the dots would disappear, the emergency would go away. I wish I'd answered his question. I realised he was waiting for an answer with content. I was being not insubordinate but disrespectful to the man.

'Casa…' I began but before I could finish he said ' Get RG in here now. Now.'

Immediately I pressed the intercom buzzer on the instrument bank in front of us.

'Yeah? The voice on the other end sounded drowsy like a bank holiday bee.

'RG. Sir wants you in the control area. Now.'

As soon as Ingrid walked in I stood up and drawled 'Of all the bars in all of Yorkshire you had to walk in…'

I was disappointed Ingrid cut me off. I'd been rehearsing the line since I was off shift.

'She with you?' said Ingrid.

'Ingrid, RG. RG, Ingrid,' I introduced them.

Ingrid didn't lock with the hand she was offered.

'I'm fed up with this dictionary I have to lug around to deal with your abbreviations,' said Ingrid, looking at me as intently as any electronic screen, 'I'm sorry you have to explain them to civilians.' She swivelled on her heels, changing course to leave.

'Ingrid, you're being rude, this isn't cool, not giving a good impression to our overseas visitors.'

'Overseas?'

'RG is from the USA. That is her jeep outside the pub. She wanted to see the moors before the heather turns. RG said we could have the jeep this afternoon, run around after lunch, local sights. She is going to bus and walk back to base.'

'Walk?' said Ingrid

'I love to walk,' said RG. 'Good for the figure too. You must walk lots,' she said to Ingrid.

'Not sure how to take that,' Ingrid came back, quick as a flash, but the warmth spreading back to her voice.

'I'd better set off now,' said RG, 'break in these sneakers.'

Both women were standing facing each other. I took each of them by the arm. – 'Sit down, have a drink.' My tone was mock movie tough guy.

A man appeared in front of us. I hadn't detected him. The pub was full of alcoves. Snug if that is what you were into.

'Everything hunky dory ladies?' Said the man, a youth really, bearded, almost, open duffel coat. Seemed the wrong sort to refer to the girls as ladies.

'Everything is fine,' I said to the young man, 'not that it concerns you.'

I stood up, my RAF uniform apparent, RG rose from her seat, her USAF uniform apparent. Ingrid remained standing.

'Can't make up your mind who to defend?' said the young man

'Are we under attack?' said RG

The youth-man radiated negativity towards us, the uniforms, the accents.

'Not from round here are you?' he said eyeballing RG and me 'and not welcome. You lot put us in danger.'

'We are here to protect everyone, including you lot' I said.

'Please don't explain the theory to him,' said Ingrid, interjecting for the first time.

'Leave it, Ingrid,' I said, 'some people can't take a drink.' I put my hand on Ingrid's arm.

'Don't touch our women,' said Duffel Coat.

'Your women?' I said, to the unlikely knight imposter.

Two more Duffel Coats emerged silently from the same alcove. They each had lapel badges on, black background, white triangle shape. I'd registered this logo in the newsreels but was too focused on the big feature to go into it. Pictures of Beatniks and Bishops marching, chanting Ban the Bomb. Yeah, I thought, I wish everyone would. I couldn't remember if they were pacifists or not. The Duffel Coat gang didn't seem that peaceful. If he touched Ingrid I wouldn't wait to find out. The atmosphere was explosive, someone was going to have to back down and..

'Everything alright here, chaps?' said a voice from yet another alcove. A tall figure emerged, then two more, V formation, the three of them stationed themselves in between us and the Duffers. The leader had an unextinguished unfiltered cigarette, and carried a rather dashing mix of tobacco, brylcreem, cologne and aviation fuel. Saviour or rival? I took in the full wings on his uniform, the other two the single wings of RAF Observers. It was RG who understood the Duffers needed to be allowed to stand down.

'I think these gentlemen were leaving, she said. Neat of them to give up their seats.'

'That so,' said the Pilot, his eyes, still bearing on the Beatniks. They said something inaudible then disappeared into the alcove. He and his crew kept them in vision until they were completely gone.

'As you were, chaps,' he said to his companions. They returned to their tankards. He then turned to RG, Ingrid and me.

'Call me Vic,' he said, 'at your service.' He shook hands with us all. I realised he was waiting for introductions.

'This is Ingrid, I'm Reginald, this is ..' It was the first time I realised I didn't know RG's name.

'And this delightful young lady?' Said Vic, taking RG's hand in a courtly gesture with a smile as bright as March moors snow. RG didn't move her hand.

'Phoney,' said Sir.

'I'm sorry?' I said. Neither of us looked up.

'Phoney war, happened before, look how that ended.'

'Everything alright Sir?' I said. 2.34 AM. I wasn't sure if it was the radar repeater that made him look green.

It was true the dots dispersed to the edge of the screen. Still discernible, still threatening, but it didn't look or feel so immediate to me.

'I don't like it,' said Sir. 'Prefer the blighters in the air.'

He wrote something on the desk. 'Take this' he said handing me a signed document. I took in the heading, special leave, 48 hours subject to recall. 'We need a contact number at all times. And that girl of yours, her name?' He took another document – some kind of list from the manacled briefcase. Seemed to me – still peripheral vision he crossed out one name at the top of the list and wrote another at the foot. 'Get some sleep, Reginald. You don't mind me calling you Reginald, do you? And I mean sleep' he said. 'You young people nowadays.'

I thought he was going to wink but he still didn't look up.

'Permission to speak, Sir ?' I said as formally as possible.

'What is it, son?' he said, 'you don't have to do that. At this hour.' He looked from the screen to the clock to me to the screen.

'Sir, I'll stay, you take the leave.'

There was a silence. I thought I might end up in the guardroom.

'Don't make implications,' he said. 'Go. Sleep. 48 hours. And when you come back bring Ingrid with you.'

'But Sir, that's against regulations.'

'Tell her to bring her passport. Photo. ID purposes only of course. Official Secrets Act and all that. Not that the most romantic of requests to court a young lady, I well know but better than…'

'Better than what, Sir?'

'Play it…'

'Cool?' I said.

'Is that the expression? Here's another for you. KBO. That's an order.' He looked straight at me.

Ingrid appeared in her Ava Gardner mode.

I managed to take my eyes off Ingrid to look straight at Vic. Vic pulled out of his wolf whistle on the first note.

She explained to RG: 'wasn't sure of the dress code. Mr Reginald Suave told me to bring my passport, we are going on a mystery tour after this.'

It was Ingrid who chose the picnic spot. Local knowledge. It was like a scene from a painting. Two men, two women, the purple moors meeting the green grass leading to the indifferent river.

'How is this river named?' Said RG

'How are you named?' Said Vic.

'Ethel Zymanski.'

'So what's with the RG, EZ?'

'Radar Girl. Christened on the VC10 over. Stuck.'

We listened to the river. RG continued 'Where I come from rivers always have the expression Mighty place in front of them, Mighty Mississippi, Mighty Hudson, Mighty Yukon…

'Esk' said Ingrid, 'River Esk. Beautiful Esk.'

The river continued without us.

'So what's the payload?' said Vic, indicating the hampers. There were two. One concocted from the base mess by myself and RG, one supplied by Bothams of Whitby by appointment to Ingrid. Vic could only get away so last minute he only had time to grab a bottle of ale on his way over.

RG seemed mesmerised by the Esk, Vic by RG. The hampers remained unopened until shadows almost reached the riverbank. RG spoke first.

'I have to check in,' she said. It was then we realised RG had a radio in this jeep, in effect a military installation, parked out of sight, out of mind.

Above the river all we heard her say was – 'Understood. Out.'

She never returned to the idyll, a wave, a highly targeted blown kiss, a cinematic screech of tyres on the track. Silence.

Ingrid covered with the transistor. 'It only receives,' she said. 'Any requests, pop pickers? Beatles or The Rolling Stones…?'

In the middle of ''A Hard Days Night'', the radio interrupted itself – 'We now go over to the newsroom for a special…'

'Turn it off,' ordered Vic, that tone which no one would countermand.

The silence returned. Ingrid and I opened the hamper.

'Breast or thigh?' she said.

'What?' said Vic. 'You know,' said Ingrid, 'that's what Grace Kelly says to Cary Grant on their picnic.'

Vic received a piece of chicken without saying thank you.

Ingrid tried to recover the tone.

'Where are you from Vic?' she said.

'Everywhere, nowhere.' said Vic, indistinct even without any chicken in his mouth.

'You have to be from somewhere. I'm from Whitby, Reginald from London.'

'Moved around a lot,' said Vic, 'RAF family.'

'North, South? You have to be from somewhere' said Ingrid.

'Beatles, Stones, breast, thigh, north , south. Why do I always have to make a choice?' said Vic.

'Easy Vic', I said. I noticed his eyes were as red as Sirs. The afternoon was slipping away as fast as the river was flowing. I was almost relieved to hear the first thunder overhead. Ingrid and I began to repack the hamper. Vic flung the empty ale bottle to the ground.

'Keep Britain Tidy' said Ingrid, 'we'll come to this beauty spot again if it's still beautiful.'

Vic picked up the bottle, for a second I wondered what he was going to do with it. The rumbling overhead intensified then seemed to dissipate in the direction of the sea.

'Vulcan,' said Vic , indicating skywards. Show's on. For real.'

The aircraft noise overhead had totally camouflaged the arrival of two military police Land Rovers.

The military policeman looked at a clipboard then at myself and Ingrid. — 'You two first vehicle. Move.'

'You, sir, second vehicle.' Vic leapt in the vehicle without opening the doors.

I helped Ingrid into ours. Her eyes remained fixed on the river as we attacked the hill.

'Nice of you to join us,' said Sir, immediately our Land Rover pulled up at Base Centre. 'RG gave me your location.'

'RG? Where is she?' We were running toward the radar op room.

'Zymanski confirmed everything. Then I put her on a VC10 out of northern sector. Smart girl. You go ahead. Alright for you young chaps.' He paused to breathe, leaning against the tunnel type wall. —'Your show this time anyway.'

I was fixed in front of the screen minutes before Sir materialized. Dots everywhere, moving, fast.

'Sir?' I said.

'Third opinion ?' said Sir. I held his glare.

'You know what to do' he said, opening his briefcase and handing me the codes. 'Do it,' said Sir.

I picked up the receiver from the desk. Sir stood behind me, his hand on my shoulder.

The receiver glowed and crackled then cleared

'V Force 1, V Force 1. Base to V Force 1 leader. Come in.'

There was a slight delay then:

'V force leader. Go ahead base.'

It was Vic. I hesitated. Sir said – 'Give him the codes. Don't think . Act.' I hesitated again. Then read the code. Vic repeated it back to me. The line was clear then crackled again.

'Confirmed' I said. Sir let go of my shoulder.

The R/T came back to life.

'That you, Reginald?' Said Vic. -Reginald, tell me about Ethel.'

'No names on this frequency' said Sir sternly, then again more softly, 'no names.'

'RG is by the river. Repeat RG is by the river,' I said.

'Understood. I will follow procedure.' A seconds pause, then 'Keep Britain Tidy.' Said V Force leader. 'Out.'

The MPs reappeared.

'You may go now, Reginald.'

'But Sir,' I protested.

The MPs guided me away along a tunnel I didn't know existed. I turned to look at Sir. There was a blinding light behind him. He smiled. 'Ingrid will be waiting. Never be rude to ladies, young man. One last thing, Reginald.'

'Sir?'

'Her name, my lady, her name was June. Since you asked. Her name was June.'

We were at the head of the passageway. There was a door like you see in submarine films. Next to it another MP had a list, headed like the note from Sir's manacled briefcase.

He checked it against Ingrid's passport and saluted me, indicating we should go through.

'We will wait for Sir,' I said to the MP.

The MP looked at his list than back to me, his red cap made him look like an automaton. 'Sir isn't on the list. You are two of the lucky ones. Move it.'

The door was closing behind us. The heather turning white.

-

4 x 4

Voluntary

'It is with great pleasure that I announce the retirement of Arthur Brice-Carrington.'

The headmaster had never liked Brice-Carrington — 'you don't understand the co in co-ed.' he once told him - and had no intention of understanding double meanings.

'Perhaps you would be so kind to step forward and accept this trophy as a sign of our appreciation.'

Arthur was kind enough to do so. Kindness, or was it self-effacement had always been one of his most evident traits.

On the dais in front of the assembly Brice -Carrington looked at the retirement gift for the first time. He had a heads up that the assembly would feature a minor presentation for him, minor was his own word, but he was unaware until this moment what form , if any a gift would take. It was a painting, a water-colour after the style of Turner, of an express, the last steam hauled service on British Railways leaving York railway station. The title was appended to the frame 'Profectionem.' *Departure*

The artist was unknown except for the initials JT frame right.

ABC as he was regularly known at High Grange looked out at the assembled boys, back at the hemisphere of masters then at the painting and out to the assembly again.

'Gratias vobis ago,' he said. *Thank you*

The gathering couldn't feel if his expression of gratitude was a pause or an ending. The silence was interrupted by the sound of one boy clapping. One or three others joined but the sound never became one and stopped in time for it to be regarded as a failure of silence rather than of sound.

A shout from a newly broken voice rang out from mid row two thirds back.

'Good old Steamy,' a reference to Brice-Carrington's private interest in steam railways.

Brice-Carrington had already resumed his seat. The headmaster, who had good reason to negate nicknames, returned to the orders of the day to come.

'Any plans, Arthur? Full steam ahead, what?' Even the second sherry among the minor gathering in the headmaster's study hardly injected any spark into the proceedings.

'Time to make tracks, headmaster.' It was the best he could do. 'Quod periit periit.' *What has happened has happened*

The headmaster moved on. Joy Waters rescued Arthur from standing alone.

'Always were a clever old buffer, Arthur. Say something in Latin everyone thinks it is profound, say it in English everyone thinks…'

'Everyone thinks what?' said Arthur, his antipathy to dangling sentences continuing to the end.

Joy never knew Arthur's secret — he had voted against opening professional staff appointments to women. If she ever found out he had prepared his answer 'nothing personal.' He didn't know why she had always disconcerted him. Or was that fascination? — that dinner at Michaelmas when she sat on his right, the guest's on the left complaint that he had not rotated his attention when the Sauternes was served still unresolved.

There was a too long silence. Arthur knew he was supposed to fill it. Was this the moment to tell her? Why would he ever see her again.

'Dr Waters…'

The headmaster made a final sweep-

'Haven't you a train to catch, Brice-Carrington? Joy, could I see you in my study as soon as possible please.'

'I have to go,' said Joy, as Arthur watched her disappear into the oak panelling.

'Be with you in a jiff.'

'Popping out, back in a tick.'

Arthur wasn't sure what people were saying to him. He'd been in the outer office for over a hour. 20 minutes ago a man with oily fingers invited him into an inner office. The two ante rooms were divided by a frosted glass door with the words Operation's Director stencilled on the upper pane. Arthur forced himself to stay. There was no retirement adjustment course. One moment he was Latin master in a private school, next he wasn't. Tempora mutantur *times change* he repeated to himself.

He could hear the trains clacking past the platform beyond – tempora mutantur, tempora mutantur - mainly diesel some steam, the sound of voices, merry on the seaward journeys, reserved or fractious in reverse. If he left the room he would lose his place. The door finally opened and he entered the Operation Director's space, an old ticket office. In the corner was an art deco hat stand. I t reminded Arthur of the head masters study the day of his interview there but now an engine driver's shiny topped cap hung where there was a mortar board.

Arthur had come a long way, waited a long time for this moment. When it came he was powerless to stop it going wrong. The Operation Director was the brusque, self-important type – nothing new in that in Arthur Brice-Carrington's old world, ' chap batting too high up the order' he thought to himself, but he wasn't sure how to play this.

'CV, P45, NI certificate, letters of reference, full disclosure clearance?' said the man.

'I thought we could have a preliminary chat, see what I can offer the outfit',

 said Brice-Carrington.

'Sorry, come back tomorrow. Paper work has to be in order. Take it from there. Good day to you, sir.'

Arthur stared at the man. He would need to psyche himself up to present himself again. He almost said ' Do you know what I have had to do to get here.' But thought better of it, the tone might be misinterpreted and he had no other plan.

Fact was retirement, life beyond the senior common room, was a struggle, a release he hadn't asked for and didn't want. He hadn't moved far from the old school but it was a more rural way of life than he had ever known. He took the cottage on the estate because it was near the railway.

The restored steam trains proudly passed by hauling the pullman buffet car specials, even the heritage diesel units had their own 'look at me I'm still working' self importance carrying longer loads of trippers from the North Yorkshire market towns to the coast. Arthur was content to watch the trains go by, the daffodils came to the embankments in the Spring, the tracks shimmered in the Summer heat, the old locomotives knew how to push aside Autumn leaves and Winter snow.

Arthur reread his books by a coal fire or summer patio. It was in the supermarket, of all places that time caught up with him.

The automated check outs were overwhelmed, the express lane too slow, as he reached the assistant on the regular line he knew he was going to be spoken to. She checked through his copies of *The Times* and *Heritage Railway* the meals from the 'Finest' range but still classed as Ready, the bottles of port and sherry without a word. As she returned his loyalty card the woman said 'ever thought of volunteering? there is a sign on the community notice board. Might get you on a different track. Sir.'

He wasn't sure what he was thanking the woman for.

The sign outside was handwritten in green ink entirely in capitals. It wasn't exactly *Metamorphoses*.

'Heritage railways need you. Keep our past alive, trains don't run by themselves, meet different people, make friends with our steam trains. Happy days, country to coast, new departures, old returns.'

Apply Operations Director.

An email and postal address was given. After the Charley Binghams fish pie, Arthur poured a Bristol Cream and composed a formal handwritten letter. He was applying to be a volunteer not Master of Balliol. He had a telephone call a few days later. The manner of the man on the phone at first call seemed business-like. Arthur took the first train the next day.

Having waited so long to meet the Operations Director he had to return home by bus the question of returning was less encouraging than the question of going for the first time. It was a matter of momentum. The epiphanic encounter at the supermarket check out taught Arthur, however belatedly that retirement was not synonymous with nothingness but a whole Novae terrae.

He was readmitted to the Director's office immediately. Arthur was loquacious, even garrulous in his love of railways generally and steam in particular. He recounted his grand journey as a young man through Europe, his holiday only last year by sleeper to the west country, the steam weekend in the Bronte country the half term before he retired, the deep dream of trans continental days to come in the observation cars of North America.

The Director raised his hand

'Transferable skills?' he said

Arthur was lost. The Director expounded.

'The term heritage can be misleading to some, the description volunteer misconstrued. This is a working transportation system.'

He gestured to the sign on the frosted glass. The word 'operations' now legible in reverse. 'You were a Latin'- he glanced at the CV — 'master.'

Arthur had not heard the word 'master' intoned like that before.

The Director continued 'what use is that?'

'I can, I am, I was, I am, I mean…' Arthur began to stammer his 'I's . It was not so much a reversion to childhood as instant dotage. The Director wouldn't help him. Arthur was obliged to continue

'I…I…I…'

'Mr…' he looked at the CV once more ' Mr Brice- Carrington, are you alright?'

Arthur looked away from the man. A steam train had pulled into the station outside the office window and whistled. Arthur didn't hear an assistant enter the office.

'This is the Way Out , sir,' she said pointing to an 1930s LNER replica sign above the outer door.

The woman at the check out regarded him with suspicion. Having given up mirrors he wasn't sure why.

'You new in these parts? Haven't seen you before.'

Brice-Carrington was about to explain the non sequitur but thought better of it.

There were only two supermarkets in this town, there was no other option regarding tuck. On the issue of introducing full automation in supermarkets he was ahead of his time. That time had not yet come.

'You alright for bags today?' He nodded, his accent unrevealed, loaded the loot into his own bag, a cross between a cricket hold-all and briefcase and disappeared.

It was a day even King Lear would be foolish to venture out. Brice-Carrington didn't care anymore. He walked the moors each day now, differing routes, low roads around the Hole of Horcum, locomotive smoke rising in the distance, high roads as taken by Postgate in the times of the Catholic persecution. Each day was different but the same. The routes were circular, beginning in his abode at first light, ending at dusk, a flask and sandwich on a good day. Wireless weather forecasts a sound of the past, seasons discernible by footfall.

The storm was coming in unbroken from the North Sea, the rain relentless, a day without daylight, who would voluntarily be on the moors at a time like this? Defeat recognised, Brice-Carrington made, crow like, for the only light in the distance. The straight line took him through rather than around becks and hollows, black trees and moss which couldn't take anymore. The swinging hotel sign was audible before it was visible.

'I would like a room for the night please,' he said to the young man on the front desk. No enquiry was made as to his credit worthiness, his baggage, his appearance. The hotel was true to the Latin root of hospitium reflected Arthur to himself looking in the mirror of the single room.

To his surprise he observed the hotel was full. There was a Christmas tree in the corner of the breakfast room but no advent calendar to enable calculations as to whether Christmas was a day away or a month away or even longer. There was no room at the tables. Guests avoided eye contact .

The young man – a badge on his waistcoat read Thomas - from the front desk assembled a card table in the bough of the Christmas tree, the shadows ameliorated by the fade / glow / fade of the tree lights.

'Good morning sir, what is it to be?' Arthur was wild-eyed. The boy continued 'full English, porridge perhaps, take the nip out of the air?'

'Porridge, yes, indeed, why not?' said Arthur.

Two further guests arrived, a man and woman, their age and relationship not immediately discernible. Was the woman the man's mother, a business relationship, something other, an April September romance? The other guests kept their eyes down, the Maitre D temporarily absent with Arthur's order.

It was the woman who took the initiative.

'Do you mind if we join you? You look as dishevelled as we do.' she said.

'Charmed,' said Arthur, standing by reflex.

'What is it, only 1 kilometer from the Youth Hostel and we still are totally drenched' she said, a fact not an explanation.

'Thomas, it would be most kind if you could procure two further chairs.'

'Porridge,' said the woman as they all sat. 'What an excellent idea.' Two steaming dishes were delivered.

The man was unshaven, but his stubble could be classed designer in contrast to the cave man style now sported by Brice-Carrington.

He spoke with his mouth full '' ..it would be most kind if you could procure two further chairs.''

'Jack please…' the woman began to remonstrate. The imitation was so perfect as to be inoffensive.

Brice-Carrington looked up for the first time. His glance at the man - not more than a boy? – coincided with a fierce upglow of the lights.

'How are you, sir,' said Jack

'John Turner, form five, not unaccomplished in the classics and plastic arts. How did you know it was me after all these years?'

'Jack these days. Beards don't change people as much as they think. You could have said ' ask' instead of 'procure' but Old Steamy…'

'Jack!' said the woman, her voice breaking the audio ceiling of the breakfast room

'Everything alright?' said Thomas.

'Hunky-dory' said Jack 'How are you keeping Sir?'

'Arthur?'

'Joy?'

'Arthur. Arthur. I'm so sorry. I didn't recognise you. Of course. How are you, how lovely to see you. I'm so sorry.'

'Merry Christmas', said Jack. 'Think I'll step out for a smoke. If that is alright by you, sir,'

It was Joy who broke the silence. 'I'm going to buy you a razor for Christmas. There is rugged and there is rugged.'

'I'll stay in the car if you don't mind', said Jack. The heater whirred with the car engine running. Joy turned the ignition off. 'I hate idling.'

'Let me see you in,' she said, taking ABC's arm.

'I'd rather you didn't,' said ABC.

'Nonsense,' said Joy. ' Nothing I haven't seen before. I'm sure.'

But as ABC opened his house door she involuntarily exclaimed.

'What happened to you, Arthur?'

'I'll be fine, I'll sort it out, meet you as arranged, back on track after seeing you.'

'You sure. I hate leaving you like this.'

'Shave, wash and brush up, good as new.'

Joy looked at Arthur for a long time. He fluffed the kiss into a hug. Arthur wished she would go, and come back after he'd tested the new razor and removed the recycling containers. She looked over his shoulder.

'You've still got it I see. The painting.' She slipped over to examine it. 'I wasn't presented with a Turner when I left.'

As the train clacked through the Esk valley Jack told him his story. It was only one term after ABC's retirement that he left to attend the local college at sixth form level. The collapse of his father's business for unspecified reasons meant he didn't stay the course.

'I wasn't sacked,' said Jack ' Pater couldn't employ any one in the paint shop, he asked me to do it. Best thing I ever did until it wasn't. Started side-lining for some business people my dad knew. Portraits as birthday presents, landscapes for your estate, nudes for…'

'In the style of Gainsborough, Turner, Hockney…'

'In the style of is what I do now, then it was…'

'Forgery.'

'Bang on. Banged up in the Open Prison outside York. That's how me and the doc…

'Doctor Waters and I.'

'Thank you…came back into contact. I enrolled in her classes there. She told me she always felt a fraud at High Grange.'

'Are you and Dr Waters involved in some way?'

'Yes and no. Coincidence, parallel lines. High Grange, local college, open prison, teacher and pupil.'

'Which way round is it?'

'This is our last excursion together. Every year the railway company offers a trip for the lads from the prison. We stay in the youth hostel near the hotel the night before the train steams in. We take over the carriages and have a guest speaker or lecturer. Music, art, geography, whatever. It's one of those things you wouldn't think works but it does. 'Not sure what I'll do when I get out, if you get my drift.'

'Et aperuerit ianuam, et clauserit ostium.' *A door closes, a door opens.*

Jack smiled at Arthur 'You know sir, I really like what you do with that,'

'With what?' said Arthur.

Jack didn't claim the idea entirely as his own. The programme was attributed to Dr J Waters, Mr A Brice-Carrington, Jack Turner with the cooperation of the Operations Director, North Yorkshire Heritage Railway and the Department of Justice under the motto Audite. *Listen*

Unofficially the Audite programme became known as 99/1. Lads talked 99% of the time, Arthur listened and gave his summary, usually one sentence, sometimes one word. The young men stood in the corridor of the old carriages waiting for their slot in Arthur's compartment. He listened to their stories of wrong turns, things they had done and regretted, things they hadn't done and wished they had, things they were going to do but decided at that moment they wouldn't. Each left the compartment with a smile. The success of the programme caused the number of trains to be doubled. Alumni of the first trains returned, often with mottos dispensed by Arthur embroidered onto their apparel in the original. As the scheme was trialled with old boys supervised by Arthur listening to old lags from less open prisons tattoos became visible with words such as Acceptio *acceptance*, Pax *peace*, Longanimatas *patience*

'So I'm your second choice?' said the Secretary of State.

'As a matter of record when I rang the office they told me they never speak of the former head master these days and there hasn't been a Latin master since… They put me onto you, first head girl ever at High Grange , Minister of Justice, perhaps the first old High Granger to be PM?'

The hesitation was audible.

'I'd be delighted' said the Secretary of State for Justice. It was estimated the *Audite* model saved scores of open and even higher security prison places per year.

'Thank you' said Joy. ' My people will send your people the itinerary. This is confidential. Surprise. '

It was Jack's idea to make more than a minor occasion. Arthur had announced his retirement on the return leg of the latest Christmas Special. The train was packed but he suddenly stood up in the buffet car and said

'When the pupils are ready the master must leave.' At first there was a silence. Wasn't there a Latin expression for this? Why go now?

Even Jack couldn't talk him out of it. When it was clear Arthur was going to stop the timetable for the final journey was devised.

The Secretary of State would arrive at York and transfer onto the steam railway at Pickering. She and an array of representatives from the prison services, his alma mater, and the railway would speak and there would be a presentation.

On the morning of the last day Arthur rang Joy and said he would join the train at his local station, Newtondale Halt. This was a request stop midway on the line where locomotives would only halt if flagged down by a passenger on the platform. Arthur deemed this to be the most appropriate point of arrival and departure.

'My mind is made up,' he told Joy in his best master's voice.

The hour, the minute arrived. The locomotive joyously approached the halt, majestically steaming, the whistle calling out. Heads contrary to regulations were craned from the windows.

There was no sign.

The locomotive and carriages dopplered past in a blur. Joy considered pulling the emergency cord. The Secretary of State's policeman deterred her. There must be an explanation. The train continued on schedule. Arthur never boarded the train at any subsequent station or the terminus. Joy insisted the policeman radio the local police to check the halt.

They received the call a hour later. A gentleman answering Brice-Carrington's description was binoculared slumped on the bench at The Halt. A rambler told the Bobby his cheery wave to a man in a tweed suit hadn't even been half returned. He assumed the man was somnolent in the spring sun. At least he had kept his feet off the seat.

The ambulance service report stated the old gent had had a paralysing stroke and was pronounced dead in the ambulance en route to the area A and E unit.

Exactly a year later Jack told the train guard they wished to alight at the next stop. As the train resumed its journey into the valley Jack patted his jacket pockets.

'I would prefer you not to smoke at this juncture', said Joy.

Jack's hands emerged with a mini-toolkit. Joy handed him the plaque. He affixed it to the bench. She read his name aloud -

 Arthur Brice-Carrington M A -

and Jack translated the solitary word of the inscription for her:

Praeceptor *Teacher*.

4 x 4

Photo: Esk valley ©HLS

Last Tape

A windowless room the wrong end of the A64.

-I'm going to miss this place, said Derek

-The place will miss you, said Eleanor

It was Derek's last day on the force. Retirement was a cottage Staithes top. Derek hated the suburbs.

-How do you want to play today, boss? said Eleanor

-It's just another day, replied Derek

-I mean the interview. She indicated the room, set up, as 1498 times before: grim , functional, airless, the way Derek liked it.

-What did you think I meant? He nearly smiled.

They entered the room in formation, Eleanor stationed in front of the voice recorder.

' 31 October 2019 , 7.45 pm, present DCI Derek Briggs, Detective Sergeant Eleanor Knight, Mr Charles Mann. For the benefit of the recorder Mr Mann is aware of his rights and is at present content for the interview to proceed without a solicitor present.'

-No brief today, Charlie? asked Derek.

-No need

-How's that then, Chaz? said Derek.

-I'm innocent. Didn't do nothing.

-Anything. Didn't do anything, Charles. For the benefit of the record, interjected Eleanor.

-Can we open a window? asked Charles.

-You into dynamite now, Charlie boy, said Derek. -What do you think this is, Grand Hotel?

When Derek started in the force in…all those years ago, Charles Mann was what then they would have called lowlife. Of course the phrase today would never be deployed, tape or not. It grieved Derek that his last case, his last day, was so, what, petty. Or so it seemed, felt to him. The series of what were classified low / medium level crimes in Scarborough town centre was a case he wanted closed fast. All due procedure followed of course, but closed, filed, and out.

Was there a pattern? The old school type smash and grab outside a mid range jewellers, a broken side window in a 4 x 4, snatched iPhone+, power tools disappearing from shop refit sites and reappearing at early morning car boot sales across county lines.

Derek was in Mann's face. – You know what the police, coppers like me, hate most?

-Me? said Charles Mann

-Don't get ahead of yourself, son, said Eleanor.

-What the police hate most is coincidence

-Coincidence?

-Yeah. You like movies, Charlie?

Eleanor ran the CCTV footage on her laptop in front of them. Scarborough never looked meaner. Late at night, early morning, soundtrack of alarms, broken glass.

-What can you see, Chaz?

-Nothing

-Exactly, we seek him here we seek him there, Charlie Mann nowhere. Look again.

In each frame a shadowy figure encircled by plastic bags.

-It's the same every time, said DCI Briggs. -Incident, alarm or 999, squad car, the homeless hoody everyone calls The Monk, bag search, zilch. The Monk describes you, adjacent before an incident, gone sharpish afterwards. We knock you up, Charlie Mann beddy-byes, couple of days later, loot sold on black market, usual outlets.

-You're just proving my point, Briggs. It's the homeless bloke, every time.

-DCI Briggs to you, you, you…

-You what?

- And don't you ever talk to me about proof.

-I've supplied you my statement. It's the homeless man. Follow the trail. Charge him.

-Charge him with what, being homeless, using non-biodegradable bags? You're using him, do you feel me, you're a, you're a…

-Easy guv, said Eleanor. Staithes never seemed so far away.

-You've nothing on me Briggs, said Charlie Mann, -everyone knows it's that lowlife, it's 'The Monk'.

-Everyone, you included, knows it's you, Mann.

There was no space between them. DCI Briggs wasn't the retiring type.

Moorish

1 August 2115. I am 100 years old.

The birthday text from the President of The Authority was functional-Present yourself to **Eternity Unit** to select options:

1 **GONA**, Go Now Age. 2 **NETA**, Near to Eternity Age.

The **E U** biomechanic assessed for option two - an offer of a thousand years. Two downsides.

'Downsides!'

'We are working on perfection. The Authority briefing is on the screen, it explains the process onto your retina reader.

The Eternity Process replaces the oxygen based blood system with nitrogen. The abbreviation is **NAP** – Nitrogen Age Postponer. You are reactivated 1000 years hence. You can stop at that time, or opt for another 1000 years forward, never back.'

'And the other downside?'

'You won't be able to cry. The nitrogen will close the tear ducts. Forever.'

As the nitrogen took effect I remembered the sound of the moor stream I knew seasons ago. A torrent in winter, a trickle in summer, the point in Spring and Autumn when the sound meant the level was the same.

'Happy New Millennia, welcome to 3115.'

The biomechanics were gathered round the **NAP** capsule like a flock of white birds.

'What season is it?' I asked, to their bemusement.

One said 'Take your documents chip and explore the facility.'

I recognised her from 1000 years ago.

I waved the chip in front of the screen.

The computer began: 'welcome to year 3115, township **YO1**, in the state of **AFTA**, the Americas Free Trade Authority'

I selected Background on the screen:

'The politics of the 21st century was characterized by referenda, the state formerly known as the UK fragmented into micro states, Scotland joining the European Free Trade Authority **EFTA**, England **AFTA**. Following Water War Three, the water rich republic of Yorkshire became a semi-autonomous region within **AFTA**.'

I asked the biomechanic if I was free to leave. Fresh air.

She almost smiled:

'You mean The Outside? We must issue you with one of these.'

It was a respirator mask, a modified version of one I'd seen on the news tube of 20th century wars.

Outside it was difficult to get my bearings. It seemed logical to believe the moor, AKA purple zone, must be uphill.

No humans, no birds, a black peace.

I pressed the info bar on my wrist map. The display in the mask eye visor read:

'In the 22nd century the purple zone was developed in line with regional policy: **HDH, LNS, FU.**'

I clicked on abbreviations. I could see abbreviations were the in thing these days. HDH = High Density Housing, LNS = Leeds Newcastle Space Elevator, FU= Fracking Units. In the endless concrete only one crack of colour, a flower, purple. It must have been all that could live out there a thousand years on.

I flung my mask into the line of the old stream The atmosphere bit my eyes. I waited for the tears to come.

Pedestal

-There are two points of view. At least. Always.

-No. There is only one. The right one.

-You mean your opinion?

-No I mean the right one. Objectively.

- I thought this was a fun day out.

-It is. I think so.

-So that makes it fun?

-Man, what is your problem?

We were standing at the foot of the statue. Above us Captain Cook was looking out to sea, middle horizon, in that 18th century kind of way. It was of its time, as, so it appeared were we.

Jaq read the inscription: 'To strive, to seek to find and not to yield.'

-Enough said, she said. Was something concealed in her parka? A hammer, paint, words. Was she going destroy everything right here right now?

-Discovered! She read aloud, a tone of voice I hadn't heard before. – Wasn't land there before he went, like all these other continents people like him went to and messed up.

I thought she was going to regurgitate her chips. Neither of us ate fish anymore.

-Leave it, I said. -Who cares now anyway. It's there, it's done. It was the way it was. Tempora mores.

-What does that mean?

There was a silence, the waves below paused, then came in again. The sun was setting over the crazy golf pitch. It was supposed to be a day to remember, nothing was meant to be serious. It was the seaside, sand not stone.

-It isn't going to stand. I can't stand it. All it represents. I'll see to it. And all the other imperialist stuff all over the hemisphere.

-You are going to be very busy, I said.

She looked at me as if everything was my fault. — Don't you care about anything? she said.

I walked alone to the bus station below. A police car blared past me on the way up. I didn't feel I had anything to be guilty about.

The Last Laugh

I always thought I knew when it would be time to stop. When the time came I wasn't too sure.

Comedy store, radio 4 6.30pm slot, Channel 4 pilot amber lit. All the time I polished my gigs at the City Varieties. Leave 'em wanting more.

The joke was me, stories, improvs, how I borrowed ever more money to pay off deeper debt. On my call centre shifts I devised an off off script where I told my life story to whoever would listen for the allotted 4 minute slot and asked them to contribute what they wanted.

The joke was on no one. Except perhaps Channel 4. Their loss was BBCs gain, the show - *Pay Back Time* went out first on BBC3, but went viral. The paradox is that after Amazon Prime bought it I was rich doing a show about debt. I knew it would catch up with me one day, but that day was as faraway as a 25% loan.

I called the house with sea glimpses The Edge.

Having to make the last Coastliner home kept my drinking under control. My agent texted me incessantly asking me if I had a new concept.

I lost the contract on my phone along with everything else. It wasn't very funny.

There was a sharp knock on the door. I owed a lot of people money, agents, dealers, satellite dish installers. Staying in bed wasn't a bad option. The noise continued.

I quarter-opened the door. It was the woman opposite. She had a London accent and had given me a piece of advice on my first day here. 'We out of towners need to make a tiny bit more effort to show we belong. Call over if there is anything I can help you with. '

I hate people who say 'a tiny bit', how could someone like that help someone like me.

I mumbled something even I couldn't catch and began to close the door.

'Are you alright?' she said, calling seasons later. My timing wasn't on enough to close the door before she saw through me into the kitchen. 'Look can you hang on for a second?'

Hang on? For what, is this some kind of joke? She returned 4 minutes later with two packages. 'Bread, still warm, 'she said, 'elderflower juice freshly pressed. It'll be a nice change for you. From the Cognac.'

'How do you know?' I said, thinking she must be another prier until I remembered that the only thing I stayed meticulous about was the recycling.

'Look it's none of my business but didn't you used to be…I'm sorry the name eludes me.'

'I still am,' I said. ' whoever I used to be.' Except I wasn't, only the name was the same, and I was being rude.

I held out my hand, 'Bernie,' I said.

Gradually I drank more elderflower juice than stuff derived from grapes.

Many loaves later Enid said to me, 'the local pub is having an open mic night. Stand up, well people doing stand up until some fall over.'

'That's so bad its good' I said to Enid, big of me.

'It's how you started isn't it? It's a way back for you, cinch with your experience. We'd be honoured if you came down. Really.'

'No. Thanks. Not what I do anymore.'

'What do you do, Bernard?' said Enid. I thought her departure, gripping the elderflower bottle rather abrupt.

At night it dawned on me what I was missing. Enid was right, should be a cinch, someone like me.

We walked to The Egton together. I can't remember the last time I was in a pub. Enid put my name down for a slot. I thought when they saw my name I might get bumped up to a feature but nothing happened. I hadn't rehearsed anything, why would I with my material?

I heard my name over the PA . As I stood upfront a brilliant light shone in my face. All I had to do was improvise. Cinch.

Looking back I realise they were quite charitable really. I knew I'd died and there was no heaven. It seemed an eternity before any regulars broke the silence. 'In your own time, chief,' or 'say something or we'll laugh.'

The next thing I heard myself say was to the barman, was it the same night?

'Brandy. Double. In your own time.'

Sands End

I say
What rotten luck
To cop it a week before the show's over
A poet and all, sensitive soul
Couldn't you see it coming?

I know
Maybe he's simply weary
Move him into the sun,
Worked before,
Bring him round?

Depends
On your point of view
Almost feel like laughing
All they've been through
To cop it a week before the show's over

Mind you,
Could almost laugh at the whole jape
Not the weeks the years
All over that mud
Can't tell one uniform from the other

But
Can't tell a soul
Poets, artists living in a hole
Could almost laugh
Almost

By
The way the sun didn't work
This time.

At Wilfred Owen plaque North Bay, Scarborough, 2019

Also by **John F King** at **York Europe Publishing:**

Wise Guy and other fables, 2008

ISBN 978-0-955851902

> **Wise Guy,** 2012, is also available as an eBook at
>
> Smashwords ISBN 9781476351735

*****Drama King**, 2010

ISBN 978-0-955851919

Funky / Guy and other micro-fiction, 2012

ISBN 978-0-955851964

Micro-Waves, 2012

ISBN 978-0-955851933

Vienna, Love, 2014

ISBN 978-0-955851971

Write Coach, 2014

ISBN 978-0-955851988

Write Coach II 2015

ISBN 978-0-9931306-1-8

A and E 2014

ISBN 978-0-955851995

Prog 2015

ISBN 978-0-9931306-0-1

What's Left 2016

ISBN 978-0-993106-2-5

Low – Rise 2016

ISBN 978-0-9931306-3-2

SW10 2017

ISBN 978-09931306-4-9

West End Story 2018

ISBN 978-0-993106-5-6

Nice People 2018

ISBN 978-0-99331306-6-3

Memories of the Future 2019

ISBN 978-09931306-7-0

The Mural painted by
Hugh Lambert Smith in 1964
in the Flying Angel, Whitby.

clock by Spiegelhalter of Whitby c1810

www.johnkinginternational.co.uk

YorkEurope2020

www.ingramcontent.com/pod-product-compliance
Lightning Source LLC
Chambersburg PA
CBHW041351010726
47507CB00002B/132